Hey, kids!
See if you can spot Santa,
Mrs. Claus, and Reindeer
hidden throughout the story.

To.........Ollie.........
You made it onto Santa's NICE list—GOOD JOB!

MERRY CHRISTMAS!

Love, from.....Grampie and Grammie

I SAW SANTA IN IOWA

Written by J.D. Green

Illustrated by Nadja Sarell and Srimalie Bassani

sourcebooks
jabberwocky

anta's not planned his vacation this year.
Mrs. Claus says, "How 'bout Iowa, my dear?
You always say it's your favorite place,
but remember, the children should not see your face."

"It's true," Santa says. "Iowa has it all:
great sights, tasty bites, fun times great and small."

Mrs. Claus says, "We should set off tonight!
And you heard what I said? You must keep out of sight!"

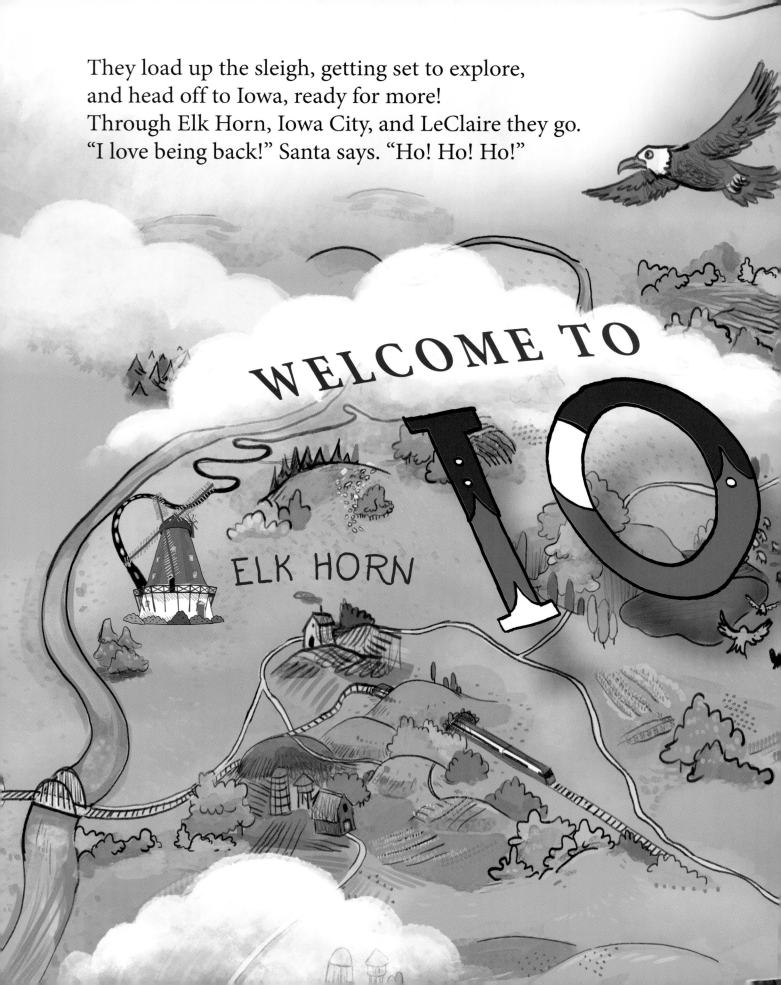

They load up the sleigh, getting set to explore,
and head off to Iowa, ready for more!
Through Elk Horn, Iowa City, and LeClaire they go.
"I love being back!" Santa says. "Ho! Ho! Ho!"

WELCOME TO
IO

ELK HORN

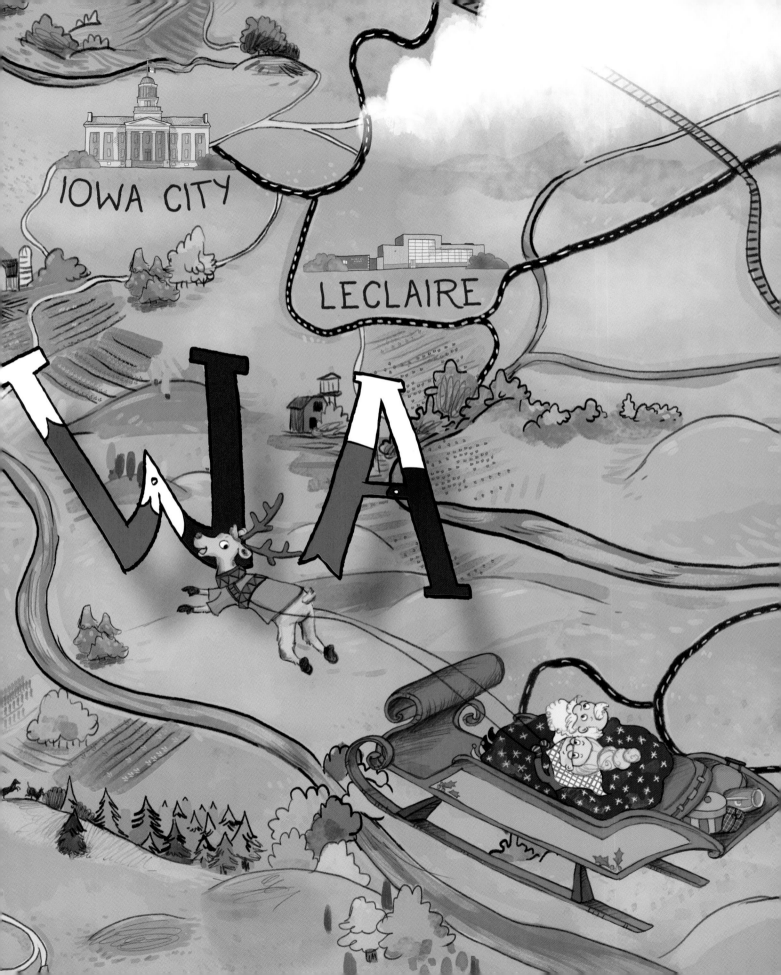

IOWA CITY

LECLAIRE

It's a family tradition, when they go away,
to buy a few gifts to remember their stay.

Smart Mrs. Claus came prepared with a list,
so first she'll go shop—not one friend will be missed!

Santa thinks buying nice gifts is quite tough.
He's feeling confused—there's just so much stuff!

His basket fills up with goodies galore,
such as sweet corn, scotcharoos, rhubarb pie,
and more.

Reindeer's not eager to stick to plans,
there's so much to see and experience firsthand!

But first he must find a good new disguise,
so he can blend in with the crowd outside!

The Clauses are done with their shopping for friends.
Now it's time to go sightseeing before their trip ends!

Back in the North Pole, Head Elf checks the mail.
He opens one letter and turns very pale…

Dear Santa,

I want to be an astronaut when I grow up.
I would love a silver space suit for Christmas.

Please.

Love, Noah xxx
Age 5
from Independence

P.S. I went to a lot of museums during my vacation and I'm pretty sure it was at The Iowa Children's Museum where I saw you playing in a rocket. Am I right?

FREEZE-DRIED
ASTRONAUT ICE CREAM

EXIT

Dear Santa,

My favorite place in the whole wide world is the ocean! Please can I have a snorkel and flippers for Christmas? Thank you!

By the way, I was at Adventureland yesterday. I didn't have my glasses on while I was swimming, but I saw someone with a big, white beard and a red-and-white bathing suit. Was it you? Please write back and tell me.

Love, Emma
Age 7
from Conrad

At home in the North, Head Elf says, "This won't do! One sighting is terrible. Now we've had two!"

Santa really should be taking more care.
It seems yet more children have spotted him there.

Dear Santa,

I would love, love, love a big, pink unicorn!
I drew one for you here.

Love, Bella x X x
Age 5¾
from Bettendorf

P.S. Did I see you at Backbone State Park,
wearing green hiking boots and a red-and-white
striped backpack? It even sounded like you were
whistling "Song of Iowa."

Am I right?

Reading the mail, Head Elf shakes his head.
This letter has caused him to turn slightly red!

Hey Santa,

Was that you at the State Capitol?
I was there with my best friend, Ben. I know you
live in the North Pole, but it really looked just like
you sitting on the bench, wearing sunglasses and
drinking a milkshake.

Oh, and we would like new baseball bats for
Christmas, please!

Bye!
William
Age 7
from Ankeny

In the North Pole, Head Elf can't believe what he's seeing!
Another TWO children have seen Santa fleeing.

Hello Santa,

My name is Olivia and I am 6½.
I love horseback riding and would like new boots
for Christmas. I went to the Iowa State Fair.

Did you go, too? I'm pretty sure I saw you
riding a horse while eating a hot dog!

Was that really you?

Love, Olivia
from Decorah

NO SLEIGHS ALLOWED

PRINCIPAL RIVERWALK

Hi Santa,

I am 8 and I would like a real duck for Christmas. My grandpa and I were watching the ducks at the Principal Riverwalk when we saw a big, red sleigh on the other side of the pond. I heard the park ranger say sleighs do not float.

Was that you?

James
from Sioux City

The vacation is over; the shopping is done.
See you soon, Iowa! Thanks for the fun!

Upon arriving home, Head Elf lets Santa know he's been spotted by multiple children. Oh no!

Emma, age 7

Noah, age 5

Dear Noah,
Yes, you did spot me at the museum! I was on my summer vacation in Iowa.

Enjoy your silver space suit.

Love, Santa x

Dear Emma,
Yes, you did spot me at Adventureland! Iowa is my favorite place to visit.

Have fun with your snorkel and flippers.

Love, Santa x

Bella, age 5¾

Dear Bella,
Yes, you did spot me at Backbone State Park! I was on my summer vacation in Iowa.

Have fun with your pink unicorn!

Love, Santa x

Mrs. Claus and Santa know just what to do.
They'll clean up this mess with a special gift or two.

When Christmas arrives, all the children who wrote
get one EXTRA gift, and inside is a note…

To my favorite child in Iowa,

On my summer break, I like getting away,
so I go to Iowa, the best place to stay.
There's so much in Iowa that I like to see,
there really is no place that I'd rather be.

So be on the lookout, 'cuz you never know,
if I might be somewhere that you like to go.
And if you have time, I like nothing better
than hearing from YOU! So write me a letter!

Merry Christmas!

Love,

Santa

XXX

Written by J.D. Green
Illustrated by Nadja Sarell and Srimalie Bassani
Additional art by Elena Rose and Darran Holmes
Designed by Geff Newland

Published by Sourcebooks Jabberwocky, an imprint of Sourcebooks, Inc.
P.O. Box 4410, Naperville, Illinois 60567-4410
(630) 961-3900
Fax: (630) 961-2168
jabberwockykids.com

Date of Production: August 2018
Run Number: HTW_PO201802
Printed and bound in China (GD)
10 9 8 7 6 5 4 3 2 1

Hey, kids! Flick back and see if you can spot Santa,
Mrs. Claus, and Reindeer hidden throughout the story.